P9-DJV-611

MAR   2007

ANOTHER DAY in the MILKY WAY

DAVID MILGRIM

G. P. PUTNAM'S SONS

For Jim, Krista and Jack

G. P. PUTNAM'S SONS
A division of Penguin Young Readers Group.
Published by The Penguin Group.
Penguin Group (USA) Inc., 375 Hudson Street, New York, NY 10014, U.S.A.
Penguin Group (Canada), 90 Eglinton Avenue East, Suite 700, Toronto, Ontario, Canada M4P 2Y3
(a division of Pearson Penguin Canada Inc.).
Penguin Books Ltd, 80 Strand, London WC2R 0RL, England.
Penguin Ireland, 25 St. Stephen's Green, Dublin 2, Ireland
(a division of Penguin Books Ltd.).
Penguin Group (Australia), 250 Camberwell Road, Camberwell, Victoria 3124, Australia
(a division of Pearson Australia Group Pty Ltd).
Penguin Books India Pvt Ltd, 11 Community Centre, Panchsheel Park, New Delhi - 110 017, India.
Penguin Group (NZ), Cnr Airborne and Rosedale Roads, Albany, Auckland 1310, New Zealand
(a division of Pearson New Zealand Ltd).
Penguin Books (South Africa) (Pty) Ltd, 24 Sturdee Avenue, Rosebank, Johannesburg 2196, South Africa.
Penguin Books Ltd, Registered Offices: 80 Strand, London WC2R 0RL, England.

Copyright © 2007 by David Milgrim.
All rights reserved. This book, or parts thereof, may not be reproduced in any form without permission
in writing from the publisher, G. P. Putnam's Sons, a division of Penguin Young Readers Group,
345 Hudson Street, New York, NY 10014. G. P. Putnam's Sons, Reg. U.S. Pat. & Tm. Off.
The scanning, uploading and distribution of this book via the Internet or via any other means
without the permission of the publisher is illegal and punishable by law.
Please purchase only authorized electronic editions, and do not participate in or encourage
electronic piracy of copyrighted materials. Your support of the author's rights is appreciated.
The publisher does not have any control over and does not assume any
responsibility for author or third-party websites or their content.
Published simultaneously in Canada. Manufactured in China by South China Printing Co. Ltd.
Design by Marikka Tamura. Text set in Equipoize Sans.
The art was made entirely with digital ink and digital oil pastel.
Library of Congress Cataloging-in-Publication Data
Milgrim, David. Another day in the Milky Way / David Milgrim. p. cm.
Summary: A young boy wakes up on a strange planet and encounters a variety of odd characters
as he tries to find his way home. [1. Planets—Fiction. 2. Dreams—Fiction.] I. Title.
PZ8.3.M5776Ano 2007 [E]—dc22 2006009154 ISBN 978-0-399-24548-0
1 3 5 7 9 10 8 6 4 2
FIRST IMPRESSION

The other day,
I woke up on the wrong planet.

I had no idea where I was, or how I got there.
It happens to me every once in a while.

I wasn't about to go to some strange school on some strange planet. But I didn't want to cause a fuss, so I played along until I could figure out what to do.

I tried to remember how I got home the other times. But the harder I tried, the more I forgot.

I asked for help, but everyone was too busy.

I started searching for a space transporter, or maybe a secret passage, or even just a rocket. All I could find was a raggedy-looking horse named Buck.

But at least he said he could get me home.

Before we had gone a mile, Buck got a cramp, and I ended up carrying HIM!

Then the sidewalk ended.

It turned out Buck wasn't a horse at all.
He was just a donkey in a costume.
His real name was Tulip.

Tulip admitted that he, in fact, had never heard of Earth, and didn't know how to get there. I can't remember what happened next, but I might have yelled a little.

Tulip called some friends. They came,
and I started to feel a little better.

None of them were real horses,
but they all had lots of advice, and pretty soon
I was more confused than ever.

I didn't know what to do. Then a tiny ant cleared her throat.

"You need to see the Starman on the Hill," she said.

Much to my surprise, everyone agreed.

I said good-bye and left at once. As I climbed higher,
the night grew darker. I had never seen so many stars,
or moons, in my life. Finally I neared an observatory on top,
and my heart began to pound.

After a search, I found the Starman on the roof.

"I've been waiting for you," he said without even turning around.

"You have?" I asked.

"Yeah, aren't you the pizza man?" he asked.

"No, I'm just trying to get home," I said.

"I hoped you could direct me back to Earth," I said.
"I'm afraid I can't even find the pizza place," the
Starman said. "That's why I have it delivered. But please
join me, it will be here soon."

The sky was as big as it was beautiful. I wondered
how I would ever find the earth in such a large place.
It all made me feel very sleepy.
Then I remembered how to get home!

It was so obvious, I don't know how I didn't think of it sooner. The gateway that brought me here was the same one that would take me home. The pizza came and I had three slices and said good-bye. Then I closed my eyes.